LUNA'S HAIR

Written by Dr Atousa Goudarzi

Illustrated by Gabriela Issa Chacón

www.caspicaarthouse.com

ISBN: 9798385832781

To our fallen blossoms

Once upon a time, when skies were
blue and trees were green, there was a
country full of happy people with
colourful dreams.

And once a month, when the full moon
shone, the women danced by the fire,
until the crack of dawn.

One woman from each tribe would
fulfil the dancers' plan, in a mystical
desert they called "Crackistan."

When the bright moon was full, the
legend then told, "Break the curse of
the land by dancing so bold."

On a cold autumn night, when the huge moon was full, the dancers felt lazy and huddled in wool.

A crack soon appeared when the earth began to shake, and hundreds of ugly Komodo dragons escaped!

The dragons were mean, with such nasty glares.
They dragged all the women by their beautiful, braided hair.

The Komodos drank in gulps and ate all the food.
They broke all the precious belongings they could!

Crawling into the crack
until the next full moon,
the dragons would return
and very much too soon.

The people felt helpless, and they also felt sad.
They could not understand what had happened to their land.

They wanted to give comfort, to cheer one another,
but most mourned alone and not with each other.

For help, many people told the cheetahs of their plight.
They promised to bring the moon down before the next full light.

One by one, from the mountain, cheetahs launched at the moon.
One by one, they all missed and sadly fell to their doom.

But, alas, a survivor was very good news!
The little baby cheetah whose name was Pirouz.

The people joined to nurse him,
this cheetah, the last.
And one man deeply loved him,
his future, his past.

But all those kind people
were still in despair! They struggled
to find some thoughts they could share.

A fisherman, nearby, then shouted
from his wagon, "Let's use the lakes and
rivers to get rid of those dragons!"

"When the crack will next open, when
the moon's in full shape, pour the waters,
drowning dragons, before they escape."

They tried to carry out what the fisherman
had taught, but the crack was much deeper
than anyone had thought!

The rivers and lakes were drained, but the
dragons survived, their black hole fed by waters
that helped them to thrive.

The people had enough! They decided to fight back!
They wanted to stop the dragons and all their nasty attacks.

They fought in the north and south, they fought in the east and west.
The plan was ever so clear, to "destroy the dragons' nest!"

They fought different battles, despite feeling so bleak,
and this challenge then left them feeling extremely weak.

The people felt helpless, and they felt very sad,
soon losing the little hope they thought that they had.

They put up with famine, they put up with rations,
but they could not defeat all those nasty dragons!

Eventually, some people decided it was time to flee,
by mountain, by sea, on magic carpets, to be free.

In hopes to remember
their beautiful land,
took saffron, pistachios
and turquoise bands.

A carpet, while flying, before the crack of dawn
carried families with children too scared to yawn.

The dragons then saw the magic carpets were flying!
They threw two big boulders at one of them, crying.

The carpet collapsed and so did its passengers.
And dragons stole belongings, just like mean scavengers.

They stole all their saffron, pistachios and turquoise bands,
while desecrating the people and their beautiful land.

Now everyone felt hopeless, and everyone was sad.
They tried to move on and forget all the bad.

In the westside, lived Luna, a courageous little girl,
who realised the dragons attacked girls' hair with its curls.

She thought, "Now, what if we cut off our hair?
When the dragons reach for us, they will grab just air!"

With all that in mind, Luna cut her long, pretty hair.
It made her feel sad, but she had to prepare.

The others followed Luna and did much the same.
Men cut women's braids as ropes, "Freedom!" they exclaimed.

Combining their ropes, gathering near, back-to-back,
a web crafted to forever close that troublesome crack.

As the next full moon shone on the
land one more time,
dragons roared out in anger and
could not commit their crime.

All happiness came back to those in this beautiful land,
each enjoying their pistachio, saffron and turquoise band.

And everyone lived in peace and harmony,
abundant as the sand.

From then on, men and women
danced under the full moon,
while singing and swaying, their
great nation forever in bloom.

Printed in Great Britain
by Amazon